Penguin Book 2475

The Foxglove Saga

Auberon Waugh, the second of six children,
was born in 1939 and educated at Downside,
where he held a scholarship in Classics. On
leaving school he joined the Royal Horse Guards.
He was severely wounded in Cyprus as the
result of an accident with a machine gun and
spent nine months in hospital. Once released,
he went to Bologna, where he wrote
The Foxglove Saga at the age of nineteen before
going up to Oxford. There he held an
Exhibition in English and briefly read Politics,
Philosophy and Economics. Soon afterwards he
joined the editorial staff of the *Daily Telegraph*,
where he spent three years before going to
France and writing *Path of Dalliance* in 1963.
Back in England, he joined the International
Publishing Corporation, by whom he is
retained as a general writer.
In 1964 Auberon Waugh moved to a large old
rectory in Wiltshire where he lives with his
wife (whom he married in 1961) and two
children. Here he wrote his latest novel, *Who
Are the Violets Now?* He relaxes by collecting
pictures and writing articles on sex, the Queen
Mother, politics and religion.